Tales of a Side Bitch

Acknowledgments

When I first wanted to write a book and do this as an author I was told it was not possible. I am blessed to understand better on my dreams. First I want to thank God, first and foremost because without him there would not be know me. My brother who was resting Nijeer Demetrius Dan Juan King. He will be forever in my heart, he was my best friend and baby brother/ 2nd oldest brother and my oldest brother Donnyell

Tales of a Side Bitch

King. My mother Kathy Crosby who has always told me when I was a little girl that I was going to be a writer. She knew her child, my dad Calvin Murph who has inspired me and all of his words for encouragement. My three beautiful children that has pushed me to be the strong woman that I am today. My Godparents Kelvin and Cassandra Riley awe man I can go on and on and on about these two but I won't I just want to say thank you father for putting them in my life. I think all of my Nijeer friends. I can't say it enough I love you all. Be on the lookout for She Wants Him but Keep Thinking of Her, and The Woman that Every Man Wants.

Tales of a Side Bitch

Intro

There was a knock at the door, for one moment I thought I was hearing something. As I walked to the foyer I glanced out the window to the driveway and saw a black on black Bugatti parked in the driveway. My heart started racing. I looked through the peep hole and did not see anyone standing there.

Tales of a Side Bitch

Who is it I yell, no one said anything. Standing there with my iPhone in my hand I dialed my sister because I became worried and she did not answer.

A key entered the door and the door knob began to turn.

I back up and my hands began to sweat and the door opens. It's Kane. He walks towards me and say hello baby I miss you with a smirk on his face because he knew I was scared. Hey honey that is not funny. I miss you too. Kane picks me up and walks me to the kitchen island while he is tongue kissing me. He pulls my clothes off and began to eat my pussy. I explode all over his face. Kane had been on tour for two months. He did not tell me he bought a new car. I dropped my cell phone and as it hit the floor I no longer had a care in the world. Popie was home.

Chapter 1

Monday mornings was always a long day. My girl AP keeps me on my P's and Q's, it is never a dull moment when we link up. The alarm rings and Kane rolled over and hit the snooze button. Kane didn't wake me because he was home from tour. He takes cares of everything. He pulls me closer to him and kisses my neck and began to massage my back. My breasts instantly become erect to his touch. Baby is it 530? I asked Kane. Yes, it is but today you're staying home with me.

The sound of his voice is so deep and sexy. My heart began to pound and my pussy felt like it was on a trampoline and butterflies was in my stomach.

Kane I have to go in today. I have a big meeting today. Nicole you own your own business so cancel your schedule. I made plans for us today. My cell phone rings. Kane grabs it and instantly turns it off. No phones today, no computers just us. I jump out of the bed and explains to him I can't baby Trenton is here with his partner and we have been planning this meeting for weeks now.

You still fucking with that cat? Kane said in a loud voice. Baby it is business and he is investing a lot of money. I can't let this meeting go.

Tales of a Side Bitch

I walk into the bathroom and turn on the shower. I glance over my shoulder just to the bed and Kane is gone.

The bathroom is all glass with a see-through shower. I lite my candles before I get in the shower and the aroma from the candles lights up the room. I step into the steaming shower and began to lather the rag and Kane joins me in the shower. He kisses my neck and I feel his manhood fully erect. Kane whisper I took care of it baby you are not going in today. I cannot do anything but listen to his demand. Kane bends me over at ease in from the back. The hot showers running down my back. I cannot resist him. He is 6'1 thick and a body that no woman can resist. We made love in the shower and then to the bed. Kane knew just how to please me.

Tales of a Side Bitch

The doorbell rings, rings, rings we both ignored it.

Kane forgot to lock the door when he stepped outside

to cancel my meeting. Someone is yelling from

downstairs Nicole, Nicole, we continue to make love

as though no one is calling out for me. All I could do

was enjoy every second of our intimacy.

AP stumps up the steps in a rage voice yelling Nicole.

I asked Kane did you go out the front door. Kane

replied yes baby why. It's AP and you did not lock

the door.

AP is standing in in the door of our bedroom and say

that's why your red ass isn't answering my calls.

I jump up and grab my robe and Kane grabs the

sheets. I closed the door. Girl we have business to

take care of today and Kane can wait. Shit, he had yo

ass waiting all this long time. AP I cannot go in

today. Why? Because Kane is home? Yes, and he

canceled the meeting and I'm sure Trenton is going to be pissed.

Trenton called me already and he is very pissed because you know what's at stake right now and you all booted and tooted. Girl just wait and let me jump in the shower down here. I have clothes in the guest room. I will jump in a car with you because my keys are upstairs and Kane is not having it. AP calls Trenton and tell him that the meeting is still on. I jump in AP 2017 BMW and mash off. I left my keys and phone to the office. AP is my BFF so she has her own keys as well. 20 minutes later we arrive at the office and my staff is not there yet. I keep a low-key cell phone in my office locked for backup. Kane has been on the road and in Atlanta he has a lot of pull. "Hot Lanta" Kane is my man, but when he is on the road I have a little fun with a guy named Shamar.

Tales of a Side Bitch

AP is setting up for our meeting with Trenton and his colleague. It is now 7 a.m. and my staff is here now. I phoned the secretary and tell her to hold all calls and buzz me when Trenton arrives. I pull out my other phone and power it on and began to use it. I needed to call Shamar and let him know that Kane is home and that I will link up with him later.

My secretary buzzes my office "yes" I answer. Trenton is here. Okay send him back. AP walks in my office five minutes before had Trenton arrives. Trenton is dark chocolate, wavy hair, weighing about 200 pounds, very cut. He walks in and I stand checking myself. AP starts laughing because she knows how fine he is. The cologne he had on lit up the hallways. I did not even notice he had walked in with his colleague.

Tales of a Side Bitch

Hello Nicole how are you? Great Trenton how are you? We hug and he kisses me on my cheek. Trenton introduced me to his partner. Nicole this is Amar who I have been talking about. Hello Amar. We shake hands and they have a seat. Nice to meet you Amar. I look at Amar and swallow with a deep breath with anguish inside. Amar and I eyes connect as if we have something we wanted to say, but the words just would not come out. The meeting lasted for about two hours. It went well and low-key phone began to ring and it was Shamar.

Nicole why you didn't tell me that you knew Trenton? I didn't know I was supposed to tell you about my business. In a smart voice. Yes the hell you should, you know damn well I have to stay low when it comes to this type of lifestyle.

Tales of a Side Bitch

Now I have to act like I don't know you which in fact I know your ass very well. Shamar I had no idea that you would be in my office with Trenton and on an alias Amar

Man Nicole I have to pull out this deal. No you cannot Shamar.

Shamar was the guy who ran the city and everybody knew not to cross him in the drug life. His money was very long and he was not the average drug dealer and not just anybody could chop it up with him. Now you know what and why this whole deal came about anyway. Shamar we have to keep it on the low about you and me.

Shamar yells FUCK Nicole I.

I interrupt him, Shamar you act as if I planned this shit out. Nicole lets meet up and discuss this. Okay babe 7 o'clock your place. Okay see you then

Tales of a Side Bitch

I walked down the hall to AP's office to let her know I am leaving for the day and I will catch the cab home. AP is on the phone with Trenton explaining to him about Kane canceling the meeting. I knock on the door to give her the signal that I was standing there. She finished up her conversation with him. What's up Nicole? Nothing I am going to head home so I'll be taking the cab and I won't be back for the rest of the day. Okay I just wanted to have the meeting with Trenton. Speaking of Trenton AP welllllll never mind I will handle that another day. Okay girl I hear ya. Call me when you get home. Okay girl talk to you later.

Chapter 2

I jump in the cab and head home. We pulled in the driveway and I noticed Kane car isn't in the driveway. I pay the cab and walk up to my door and grab the spare key in the flowerpot and go inside. I walk upstairs to look for my phone to call Kane, but it was not where I left it. I call AP off the house phone to let her know I made it home. I ring Kane but no answer. It was now 5 PM and still no Kane I figure he was gone this long because he was mad about this morning. I called Lexi on the low-key phone to let her know that she has to be on time today with the draw. Lexi is the girl that works for Shamar that does all the money drops.

Shamar runs a mob down in Vegas and I make sure everything is on schedule for him. I hear keys rumbling downstairs and I knew it was Kane. He walks up the stairs I hang up with Lexie and hurry and hide the phone. I greet him with a kiss and sucked his bottom lip as I pull away hoping that there won't be tension between us, but it didn't work.

Tales of a Side Bitch

Why did you go in against what I asked you not to do? I step back and say baby I told you that was a very important meeting and Trenton had a lot of money on the line. We have been planning this meeting now for some weeks. I called and called you to see when you were coming back off tour and scheduled this around us, Kane replied in a strong voice

THIS HAS NOTHING TO DO WITH ME. Whatever Trenton was giving you I could gave that to you.

Maybe this isn't just about money, he is investing a new project that will launch next month and this project would have us set for life. Set for life Kane ask….

I told you to never fuck with that cat….

I didn't, but when he came to me about the idea I called you.

So how much this cat is investing Nicole?

Baby $90,000

So wats the cut off this deal?

Baby let's not discuss Trenton and work

I unzipped his pants and pulled out his dick and began giving him head to take his mind off of what took place today. And it did.

All I wanted to do is keep my man happy. Kane looked down at me while I was stroking the shaft of his Dick giving him head.

Nicole you know I love you

I look up at him with a sexy look and say it back and put his nuts in my mouth. All I could hear was Kane moaning while I suck all the juices out his body and swallow. Before he could nut I took off his shirt and grabbed him by his hand and lead the way to our bedroom. I removed his shoes and he took off his pants. I turned on some music and push him on the bed. I climb on him and kiss him from his head to his Dick. Kane nutted in my mouth and I swallowed all the cum that came out of him. I love giving him what he wants when im intimate with him. I got his Dick rock hard again and we make love for hours. Now that Kane is off to sleep I go downstairs to cook dinner and began to look for my phone. Kane had it locked in his car. I go upstairs to get the keys. I retrieve my phone and I had six missed calls and 20 text messages. I am back and sigh I hear a phone ringing, at first I'm thinking it's his phone and then all of a sudden it hit me. That it was my low-key phone. I run upstairs and try to retrieve it and realize I tossed it under the bed and Kane is on the side that side of the bed. I tip toe around him and grab it and run downstairs to the guest room. It was Shamar "shit I forgot I was supposed to meet up with him" I whisper in a low but mean voice. Yes and hit the end button by mistake and

He calls back and I answer in a low tone voice. Hello. He Yells Nicole Nicole ….I pause and don't say anything he yells Nicole, and I say in a low voice Hey Shamar. He yells where are you? I reply I have to meet you another time, Sorry Shamar I can't make it. Why not? I told you earlier that Kane was home and I thought I will be able to meet up, but I just can't right now. So you set this shit up Nicole and make me wait. Shamar I gotta go.

I turn the phone off so that no more calls can come through and not to mention to hide the damn phone till I get back to my office. Before Kane finds out. I run down to the basement and stash in the bookshelf in the office. Dinner is done so I wake Kane up for dinner. When he was done I washed up and climb back into bed. I kiss him on his soft juicy lips and play with his ears with my tongue down to his chest. I tease him for a bit before his manhood raise again. I grab his balls with one hand and his dick with the other hand tease him before I put it all into my mouth. I never had a problem pleasing my man because he takes care of home and took very good care of me. He is so damn sexy and I made sure he didn't need to pussy from anywhere but home, but he is always on the rode so to make time pass for me I keep busy with my company that was built from the ground and is doing very well.

The next day I meet up with AP and move some money for Shamar something I don't do. This was something that Lexi did but for some reason he wanted me to do it on this particular day. I call Shamar off my low-key phone to discuss the details of this and what was it okay if AP came along. Shamar said no, Nicole you know I don't want your home girl to come with you. I leave a piece by a meter? At his mansion. When I pull up I noticed that it was no cars in his driveway. I put the code in the gate. Now my mind is wondering even more. I get out of the car and head to the door, but before I can push the doorbell Shamar opens the door. He snatched me by my arm and slams the door.

Nicole what the funk is you thinking? What do mean and why you handling me so rough? Check this out when I talk to you did you really think I wanted you to run some money when I got Lexi?

Tales of a Side Bitch

Well you know Id asked myself the same question but I know not to question you.

Nicole what am I going to do with you? You have me in a rough spot. I don't want just your time or any of this whatsoever I don't even want you working in these streets anymore. What does that mean?

Nicole listen have you talked to Trenton since the last meeting? No not since Kane came home. Speaking of Kane, Nicole you got to choose.

What you mean choose Shamar? He is never there for you only when it's convenient for him. You are Smart very talented. Shamar you are stepping out of line right now. You knew what I had going on. I love him and we both agreed that this would never be a conversation for us and now you want me to choose. Shamar I can't and I would not so let's get back to business. Trenton does not have to know about you.

Tales of a Side Bitch

The money is up in the paperwork is signed. All that is left right now is for the manufacturers to finish with the drawing.

Nicole are you listening to me?

Yes, I am listening to you, but did you hear me when I say I'm not choosing? Okay I have some thinking to do. His phone rang. He answer his phone and go into the next room to talk. I pull out my phone and text Kane I am on my way home and I'm just leaving from the bank. He replied back make sure when you get home to be naked for me when I get there. I smile instead and sent a :-) back. Shamar returns to the room and grabs me and kissed me on my lips. My heart drops because I knew I couldn't have sex with him. I pull away and said I can't Kane would kill me. Shamar grabs me and say fuck Kane you're my bitch. We began to argue and our conversation got very heated. I grabbed my keys and leave. As I headed to the bank I was in a daze all the way to the bank and all the way home. Trying to wrap my head around what just took place. AP was blowing my phone up but I couldn't answer.

I get to the house and sit in my car parked in the driveway just thinking. I did notice that Kane had pulled up. He walks over to the car and opened the door. Baby what is wrong? Kane asked me. I was startled because I didn't know notice him. I get out of the car kisses him and say nothing baby how was your day? Good just at a business meeting all day but how was your day Cole? It was good I guess. You guess? Yeah it was good. Why are you sitting in the car in the driveway? I was on a conference call. No you were not because when I opened the door it was like you seen a ghost you didn't have the phone in your hand.

I had just finished up the call when you open the door.

We both walk up to the door Kane sticks his key and opened the door. Oh shit in a low voice.

Kane ask? What's wrong?

My laptop is in the car. Okay I will get it for you. Thank you honey. I kickoff my heels and plowed on the couch. Kane walks in and sit the laptop on the table and starts rubbing my feet. Baby will you start the shower for me? Yes, Kane walks up the stairs and start the shower and lite my favorite candles. I pull out my low-key phone and check on Lexi to make sure she dropped the money and that it was on time. Lexi text back done. That it was done and that was a big relief because I was worried about that too. I turned the phone completely off and stashed it in my purse. Kane comes downstairs and start asking me about my day again. I knew he didn't believe me about the conference call. Baby my day was great. I'm just tired now and now that I'm home with you I'm even better. Kane phone rings so our conversation was cut short and I was happy about that because I didn't care to talk about especially because he has something to do with Shamar and Him. I head up the stairs and get into the shower on the bed it was a card and a black box. The card was handwritten and it said

Thanks for coming into my life, I want to know will you be my wife? There isn't a day I think of you and when I'm not around I see my angels to watch over you.

Tales of a Side Bitch

I blush and open the box and it was empty with a big smiley face inside and I go and get in the shower all tingly inside. I hopped in the shower and the steaming water run down my back and all I could do was think about what Kane had just done and my situation with Shamar. I wanted to block it all out and focus on my relationship and business but I just could not. I loved Kane and there was no way that I was leaving him for Shamar. Right then it hit me and I realize he was just too much for me. I get out of the shower and climb into bed and doze off to sleep. Kane wakes me and asked baby are you okay? I replied no

Talk to me baby. It's my job and all the things that is going on. We need a vacation.

That is why I didn't want you to go into work. You work too hard. Honestly I really don't want you working at all.

Baby I know but this is the only way I can pass time when you're not here. Kane asked me about the card and box I began to blush because I knew what he was getting at. Baby I love the card, but what was the box about? Are you trying to trick me? No Kane replied. Baby I want you in my life forever. As we continue to talk I doze off again but this time in his arms. He was always here when I needed him. He was my lover, partner and best friend.

Chapter 3

Thinking about the argument – Shamar and I had so had to set things straight with him. I get into the office and put up my low-key phone. I noticed that AP was not in yet and this was unusual so I figure she was on her way. An hour had passed and she still was not in. I asked my secretary to ring her and she did not answer. I hit her up and still no answer. I tell my secretary that I will be back and take all my calls.

I pull up to AP house and Shamar cars parked outside. My heart drops and I pull off and head back to the office and pull out my low-key phone and call show Shamar. He answer "yeah" I look at the phone with a frown. Hey Shamar what's up? Nothing he replied back. Where are you? Home why, oh nothing I just got into the office and I wanted to touch base with you about last night. Okay, Shamar replied. He was very short and to the point. We hung up and I power off the phone I buzz AP again but she does not answer I asked myself should I ask her or just wait till the time is right. I decided not to say anything to her. It was now 10:30 a.m. and AP walk into the office. Hey girl I swallow and check my tone of voice. Hey AP I wanted to say something but I didn't want her to know I saw Shamar car parked to her house. AP did you give the manufacturers the drawings yet? Yes, I did yesterday, but Trenton has to sign off on them and everyone else has signed except him. Okay will you fax it over to him so we can get the ball rolling? Sure are you okay Nicole? Yeah I'm fine (deep down I really wasn't) AP leaves my office.

I try to do some files to try and drown out my thoughts. I realize I had two meetings today so I buzz my secretary and explained to her that I need to take a vacation and to use the business account to pay for it. It is now 2 p.m. and I am ending my meetings for the day and I no longer wanted to set shit up for Shamar, but first I must find out the deal with him and AP. She is my best friend but she never mentioned she knew Shamar to me. Now I'm all wrapped up to find out what them to has in common. Kane is out of town doing a show so now I can do some investigation. It's now eight at night and I head to the office to see what she has in her office. I park in the lower level of the parking garage and check to make sure the security was in the area so that I could hit up. I enter my office and take down a picture I always notice her fixing each morning and behind it was a key. I always knew about the safe behind the bookcase but never once thought to go in it. I put the key and open the safe. I really wasn't ready to find out what I needed to know. There were two big boxes that said first and second. I was puzzled because she never told me about these two boxes. So I decided to open the box that said second first. There were receipts and pictures in the bottom of the box and another small box with the baby picture any with her and Shamar. My heart drop, my feet got kinky and my hands began to sweat. I knew of her baby that passed away, but we never discuss who the father was. That was five years ago. I close the box and put it back into the second box and put it back into the safe. I open the box that said first. At this point I did not want to open it." Here we go "I open the box and each photos of her and she Shamar and more items that were connecting them together. I shove everything back into the box and close the safe and put the key back and leave out her office. Now I'm sitting at my desk with my low-key phone in my hand thinking should I call him or AP and either way I needed to know about these two. I call AP with my main phone and set up a girl's night with her because there are some things we need to know and tell one another. After our conversation lasted on the phone about 30 min. I hang up with her and go back to her office and make sure everything was in place.

Lexi call and tell me that she needs off this week and can I get a replacement.

Yeah Lexi I got you. I call Shamar to tell him that Lexi is off for the week and that I will be handling the runs.

Hell nall Nicole, Shamar yells you are not doing no runs and I told you that once.

Shamar you have been working Lexi nonstop so let the girl have some time off.

Shit Nicole you are hard headed damn. Lexi gets paid damn good. She doesn't need no day off. All she does is drop and keep it moving.

Shamar you at like I don't know how to handle shit till she gets back.

Tales of a Side Bitch

Nicole you take the week off to Lexi gets back and he hangs up the phone. I called right back but get no answer. I hopped in my 2016 infinity truck and drive over to his crib. I didn't like how he handled me and my mind is already racing about this shit I just saw with him and my best friend. Normally I was set up a time and go to his house, but at this point I need to see him. I buzz the gate and he let me in. As I'm walking up to the door he is standing out on his porch smoking a blunt.

What brings you by Nicole?

So this how you greet me now. He turns and walks in the house. I followed him and he puts out his blunt and turned to me and say

I told you to take the week off and you fly over here for what?

Tales of a Side Bitch

I need to know who you are going to have handling shit while you're on your period because I do not want to be cleaning up shit behind someone if they fuck up.

I got this Nicole you don't have nothing to worry about. Have a seat.

Nall I'll stand. Shamar only has on his boxers and a white beater.

He walks up to me and kissed me on my lips. I'm dressed in a white sundress, he grabs my ass and all I could do was kiss him back because he had me so tight. I melted because he is smelling so good. Even if I wanted to push him off me it wasn't happening. He grabbed my pussy and began to play with the head with one finger. I was already wet from his touch. I pulled down his shorts and started caressing the chef of his dick. It was already rock-hard. He turned me around and bend me over his all-white couch and slide on a condom and push inside of me. All I thought about was him and AP at that moment while he is hitting me from the back. I enjoyed it all at the same time. I wanted to break it off with him but at that moment the way he made me feel, it was all to right.

The next day I felt some kind of way and I knew I needed to make some decisions because he wanted too much for me. On the way to the office I was listening to Keith Sweat new single so it could put me in the mood I needed to be in. I called Kane to tell him good morning and how much I miss him. He answers hello baby girl and all I could do was cry. Baby what's wrong? The phone went silent he listened to me cry. Baby girl talk to me. Kane I miss you.

Tales of a Side Bitch

Baby do you want me to fly you in so you can take a mini vacation while I'm handling business. I told you to come (the phone's silent) It's more to why you are crying I know you. Talk to me. You know I don't like to hear my queen upset. Listening to him call me his queen makes me even harder to talk because he is out of town doing his thing for us and I'm fucking up and cheating. I wanted to come clean, but the words just could not come out.

Do you Cole?

I replied yes baby. I just have to get away let me call you right back so I can make reservations for the next flight out.

Okay baby. I hang up the phone and call show Shamar to let him know it was over between us. He didn't take it good because he had just fucked me. His last words were" Nicole this isn't over "at that point I didn't care about him and AP anymore well at least for now I didn't.

Chapter 4

I listened to Kane so while on the plane all I could do was think about all the shit I was going through and Kane had no clue to any of the madness that was going on. I knew I had to come clean about something or Kane was going to drill me all night, but all I wanted to do was lay in his arms and forget about everything. I landed hour later and Kane was waiting for me at the airport and I hugged him so tight I couldn't let go. We get back to the hotel and I unpack my bags and he start the questions like a drill sergeant. All I could do was tell him baby I wish I had listened to you. Listen to me about what? About Trenton. Okay what's going on? I just don't feel right about the situation. He didn't do anything; I just don't feel right about this.

Give him back his money and tell him the project didn't go through or they couldn't make it.

I wish it was that easy

Let me think of something Cole but right now I'm glad you're here with me. I am too baby. I get into the shower and he had my favorite candles already in there waiting to be lit and I turn on Pandora and mellow out all the thoughts and relax my mind. I lean out the shower and text AP to let her know that I'm out of town and I should return in a week. She didn't respond back and it was late so I expected that. I shut off my phone and finished up my shower and climb into bed with Kane and lay on his chest. He grabs a hold me as if I was a newborn baby. I could hear his heartbeat. I felt so much security and I had no care in the world once again at that point. He kisses me on my forehead and began to rub me down. I dozed off to sleep. He wakes me up by eating my pussy. I tremble to the stroke of his tongue. This man had a mean head game on him I climaxed three times and when he came up I returned the favor. He put his nuts on my chest and I play with his jewels and teases the moan that he may was very sexy to me. He nut on my lips and I love every drop that skated out. I wasn't finished with them just yet I played with his head and let his dick touched the back of my throat till it was all of his 8 ½ inches long. Yeah his Dick was big. He was a manse so whatever he wanted I did it to make him happy. The fact that I cheated on him is killing me inside.

The next morning, we went out for breakfast and then shopping. My phone was still off but it was no need to turn it back on. He had a show that night at a strip joint. I get dressed to join him by his side. We are in the club popping bottles and enjoying the night. The club was pack and Kane was lit from all the liquor that he had consumed from that night. After the show we get into the limo and head to the studio. He is ready to lay some tracks and smoke with his fellows. I pull out my phone and powered it on and I have 15 text messages and 18 voicemails. I checked my emails and the manufacturers had emailed me about the project I wanted to call Trenton and let him know, but I didn't want to upset Kane so I waited until later to do that.

Back at the hotel and Kane is knocked out so I hit up Trenton and give him the details and what needs to be done. I kept it short because I didn't want him asking too many questions. I call AP the next to check in to make sure she has everything taken care of. She did

not answer so I left her a voicemail, she sent me a text

"I got your back"

Time is winding down and he did all his shows. We

pack up and I am gain for heading home but that is

not what he had planned. We fly out to Vegas to the

most beautiful hotel   it was very

nice. He wouldn't let me leave his sight so calling

Shamar was out of the question especially now that I

broke things off with him. We still have business to

take care of. I had thought about calling Lexi but that

was out of the question as well. I just cannot let him

know about the mob that I help run down here in

Vegas. We walked a strip and I run into Lexi I look at

her and say Lexi? She looks at me as if I was not

talking to her

Tales of a Side Bitch

Lexi what are you doing down here in Vegas?

I pull her to the side and demand an answer.

Nicole we have not heard from you in a week so Shamar have someone else

Running the calls now. Shamar told me that you were

No longer a part of his team I wanted to call you and ask

What had happened but he always told me to never ask

Or check behind him……... Okay Lexi

I will call you in an hour so stay by the phone…….

Okay Nicole……. Oh and by the way Lexi do you know anything about AP and Shamar?

Tales of a Side Bitch

Nicole I cannot tell you. That is none of my business

Kane stops to the bar to get a drink and while I was chopping it up with Lexi.

She walks off.

Baby I am tired. Do you want to leave? You can stay I'll call the driver to drop me off. No I will go with you. Kane and the driver dropped me off to the room and I ask is if I'm going to lay down until Kane leaves back out as I hear the door shut I jump up and grab my low phone and phone Lexi to drill her about what she knew but no answer. I call Shamar and he answered with an attitude.

How are you? I'm cool what's up?

So I'm no longer part of your team?

I have not heard from you in a week and

Tales of a Side Bitch

You storm out like a bitch and then you tell

Me we are done. Business don't stop because

You are in your feelings. Okay so this is it Shamar?

You tell me Nicole. I'm not going to stop moving

Because you tripping. It's very clearly who you chose "Kane".

I'm cutting ties so what else do you want?

What about our business agreement? That still on point so holler at me about that.

Okay well you have a good day. The conversation ends and I lay across the bed and think about him in AP and why she would hold out on me about them two. I wasn't mad about the decision that I made because I love Kane and that was who I wanted to be with. I throw my low-key phone back in my suitcase and jump in the shower. My cell phone is ringing but I couldn't answer so it rings again. I hop out of the shower and grab my rope. It was AP so I called her back. She is all excited to hear from me and so was I because I had missed her and we usually have our girls' day each week and we talked for about an hour. We laughed and laughed but I was hurting because she was still holding out. After our call I began to cry because she is my best friend and I couldn't understand why she wanted to hold some important information from me. It's now 2:30 AM and Kane gets in a go straight to the shower.

Chapter 5

Tales of a Side Bitch

The next morning Kane took me to his family house in Vegas and out to eat. His phone rings and it was his manager letting him know that she booked him for three shows down in Atlanta in the next two days. I was happy because I was ready to go and get back to work. We fly out the next day. I enter my office there were cards and flowers on my desk. All my employees have missed me. My day got started lovely. I was thinking should I keep my low-key phone or turn the service off. Some odd reason I felt the need to turn it on. A text messages from Shamar saying he needed to talk to me and it was an emergency. I wanted to ignore the text but he said it was an emergency. I needed a meeting with my staff so after the meeting was over I continued as if nothing has happened. AP and I had our girls' day as usual and we talked and laughed. Kane was leaving back out in a few days and I can't wait. I love that man so much and he means the world to me. We leave the spa and head home. I like my candles in the house and turn on some Marvin Gaye to relax my mind. I turn on the TV, but mute the sound and noticed a picture of Lexi on the screen. I run turn down the music and rewind the news back to hear what it was saying. Lexi was murder and they are looking for some suspects. My heart drops and I began to cry because Lexi was a good girl and I'm sure it was mistaken identity. My phone rings and its AP girl did you see the news?

Yes!

I am heartbroken she was a sweet girl and all she wanted to do was have a modeling career I know my other line beeps and it was an unknown number. I almost didn't answer. I click over in his Trenton and he say three words to me

Office one hour

I clicked back over and finish talking to AP we both were in disbelief because we knew her personally well at least we thought we did. I hung up with AP and jump in the shower and change into some casual clothes. I head to the office and wait for Trenton. He calls me to let him in and before I could say anything he say Nicole this is why I asked you to find her

I knew this would get very ugly

What happened to Lexi Trent?

Man that bitch stole the money and she tried to leave for Mexico. They caught her in Cali where she always goes to get away. She was packing and they rolled up on her. They? Who is they?

Tales of a Side Bitch

Nicole just stay clear of all this. Do not call my phone or Amar. I'm waiting on my other phone to get here. My phone ring in his Kane hello baby how are you I'm at the office finishing up some paperwork. Where are you baby? I'm home. Home, I yell. Yeah what's the problem nothing I just wasn't expecting you for another two days. Yeah one of the shows got canceled so I took off on the first flight back. Okay I'll be home shortly. I hang up with Kane and finish with Trent. So what now

I have to hit up Marty to count the money to make sure we still on point. Hague is in Vegas and I need to chill till this shit die down right now. It's too hot about Lexi so let me handle this and I'll get back with you.

We leave the office and I head home to what's more important. Lord knows that's where I need to be with all this craziness going on. Kane is cooking dinner and I'm ready to get my back blowed out. I go upstairs and change into something romantic. I like to role-play with him but right now I want to get straight to it. I set the table with wine glasses and candles. He smacked me on my phat ass and kissed me down my neck and I instantly got wet. He whispered baby you going to let daddy get that ass tonight? Yes, Poppie. He sucked the lobe of my ear and walk away. I served him his food and sit on his lap and start talking dirty. I wanted his food LOL he instantly rises up. I remove his shirt and kissed him passionately down his chest. He loves when I play with his nipples. He picked me up and walked me to the Livingroom. While he is walking he is dropping his pants. I'm all hot and ready for Popie to put me on 100. We kiss and I'm talking dirty. He put my legs in a V and kiss and lick my ass. His tongue flickering like a snake from my pussy to my ass. I'm playing with this nipple and he stands up and get the KY and slide in my ass slowly but firm. I scream of pain, and it feels like flames of fire running through my body. I grabbed a pillow and cover my face and hold it for dear life. He pushes real slow and is finally all the way in. I relax and try to enjoy. I couldn't run because he had total control of me. He plays with my click with one hand while he strokes my ass. I enjoyed him and the pain all at the same time.

The next day for some reason AP and I walked through the office halls and it felt very strange so finally AP say can we talk? Yes, girl you know I'm always open to my BFF. Now or later? Now. We walk in the office shut the door and AP bites her lip and mumble I don't know how to say this say what?

Tales of a Side Bitch

Just say it. Well remember I told you that I had a child that I lost in that I did not know who the father was or maybe never mention the father to you? Yes. Well I knew all along I just didn't want no one to know. The guy is Shamar I wanted to tell you but I didn't want to relive my past. I know about you and him Nicole "what "why you didn't say anything AP? Because he asked me not to and I didn't want to hurt you. What do you mean hurt me? That's your baby daddy and I would never have been with him.

I know but Shamar is a different kind of guy and if he wants something he goes and get it.

I found out about you and him when you were in Jamaica with Kane. AP that is over two years ago and you kept this from me all this long time? Nicole he threatened me I didn't want no one hurt.

Tales of a Side Bitch

I can't believe this AP you are my best friend and we don't hold secrets especially something like this.

I know and that's why I'm coming to you now

I sit back in the chair and began to think. Should I tell her that I went through her lock box? I grasp with a deep breath and it rolled off my tongue. I have something I want to tell you. The other day when you came to work late. I called you and you didn't answer so I went to your house to make sure you were okay. When I pulled up I saw his car so I just pulled off. I cannot face the truth or find out what or why he was at your house. What was that all about AP? The room goes silent. I sat there waiting for an answer from AP and it finally rolls off her tongue. I slept with him I did not want to because I knew about you and his situation but I knew you loved Kane. I just wanted to feel loved again. Wait I do love Kane no doubt but why do it with him AP? It was only sex I don't want

him. I would never sleep behind your back and is

respect AP.

I'm sorry and I feel terrible about all of this. I don't

talk to Shamar anymore because he wanted me to

choose and that was very crazy. I stare out the

window with my arms folded thinking. AP walks

over and put her arms around me. I turned to her and

hug her back. I wanted to tell her everything but I just

couldn't. AP asked you mean to tell me he let you

leave him so easy. He was upset but at the end of the

day he knew what time it was. I can't worry about

how he feels when I shouldn't have been with him in

the first place. I changed the subject and asked her do

you have any meetings tomorrow? Yes, at 1 PM okay

I don't have any so I will be out of the office so if you

need anything to call me. I'm going to leave for the

rest of the day as well okay talk to you later. My mind is racing and all I could do is think about the morning Kane turned off my alarm clock and my hardhead did not listen.

I call Kane

Hello baby, hello baby girl what are you up to baby girl? Nothing what are you getting into

Getting ready to go into this meeting with some top guns.

How is your day? Good baby just missing you as always.

I know baby I'll be home later tonight

Okay I love you a lot. Love you too baby girl later

We never say goodbye to each other because that means we will never see one another again. I want to tell Kane everything but I know he would not take it lightly about me cheating on him and I can't blame him. I know sooner later I would have to tell him but for now I'm zipping my lips. I'm leaving the office and I forgot that I needed to stop to the grocery store and pick up some milk and eggs for breakfast in the morning. I decided to call Shamar because I needed to know what was going on with him. I call his phone private from my phone but no one answered. I call AP and tell her to change the alarm at the office which that is something I never do but for some odd reason I needed to. I put up the groceries that I purchase and lite my candles and go down to our office in the basement and fax some papers that Kane had left for me to do for him. I ordered some pizza for the night because I did not feel like cooking. I poured a glass of wine so I could relax and wait for my Kane. I fall asleep waiting on him and its 3 a.m. and I roll over and noticed he is not in the bed. I grabbed my robe and go downstairs and Kane shirt is laying across the kitchen chair so I go into the office and Kane is sitting in front of the computer drinking. I walk to him and lean over and kiss him he kisses me back and say Nicole do you have something you want to tell me? I instantly ask him what was on his is mind because I didn't want to start telling on myself. Nicole I'm going to ask you one more time is something you want to tell me? Now I'm nervous because Kane never talk to me like this. Baby I don't know what you are talking about. Kane slams his hand on the desk and say have you been fucking around on me Nicole? I instantly faint because I don't want to lose him over Shamar. When I woke up Kane was still sitting in the chair but I was lying on the couch in the office. Kane say I'm ready to talk when you are. I sit up asking what was going on. Kane ask are you okay and I reply yes. Okay now tell me are you cheating on me? My hands and feet start to get sweaty and hot and my heart starts to pump fast out of fear. Before I start Kane I love you and there is nothing or no one in this world I want. He just sits there and when Kane is silent it is not a good. Baby I did cheat but it was only brief. I was missing you and needed someone to talk to. Kane stands up and start yelling and we get into this big argument and the last words I remember him saying was what goes around comes around and I could not get that statement out of my head. I wanted to just hug him and wish this was never an argument but Kane pushes me off him. I knew at that point I had fucked up. Kane asked me did you fuck him. And what was his name. I never told him his name but I was real about our sexual encounter.

Tales of a Side Bitch

Over the next two weeks Kane slept in the guest room. It was so different because he was so secretive now and I hated it. I flooded myself with work to try get my stuff together because I had not had sex in two weeks and that was driving me crazy. AP and I hung out and we talked about what happened with Kane and me and how I needed sex. AP could not believe that Kane found out about me cheating and I was dying to find out how he knew or found out. I told AP I need her help because I need to know who would try and end my relationship with Kane we had a plan and decided to executed the next day after we got off from work. I put out my mind what happened to Lexi because I did not want shit to do with that. My secretary buzzes my office and tell me that Amar on the line. Okay thank you

Hello Amar this is Nicole

Tales of a Side Bitch

How may I help you?

I received a letter today from Nijeer enterprise that
the contract has been cancel.

Yes, it has Mr. Young.

Can you tell me why?

Well when the check bounced we decided to not
move forward.

It was a lot of money on the line.

And for the check to bounced we normally charge
you for a fee

But if you notice in the letter we did not

Charge you any fees and just canceled the contract

Nicole why you acting like a bitch.

The conversation turned from professional to personal

Mr. Young I apologize but if you continue this kind
of language

I'll have to terminate this call

Tales of a Side Bitch

Mr. Young hangs up.

I buzz my secretary and tell her from now on only take messages from Mr. Amar. After the conversation with Shamar I knew this was going to turn sour. I did not call Trent to tell him about the contract but all I wanted to do was get shit right with Kane and I. He told me not to mess with him and I did not listen. "Your man would never steer you wrong was the thoughts that was going through my head "Trent was out of town laying low and I would think Shamar would be doing the same thing but he's on some other bull shit and now it's money involved but I'm not the one who took his money so I don't know why he is all mad at me. I call Kane to try and talk to him but he forward me to the voicemail. I call him again and still no answer so I send him a text and he reply back this time. Kane I love you and I'm very sorry baby.

Tales of a Side Bitch

I would do anything to make this right.

He texts back was done is done.

I did get some relief that he did text back. I send him one last text baby we need to talk and I'll be home in 30 minutes. He didn't respond back but I didn't mind because I know I was wrong and I had to make things right. 30 minutes later I am home listen to Pandora and cleaning with dinner on the stove I have so much to say to Kane. Hours had passed and Kane is now home. The food is getting cold and I can imagine him just leaving and not saying a word. I go upstairs and look in the closet and all of his things are still there but his suitcase is gone. I go to the guest room where he had been sleeping and it was a note on the bed. I didn't want to read it because I thought it was his goodbye. I sat on the bed and read the note and it says

Tales of a Side Bitch

Nicole I went to Miami and I'll be home around noon tomorrow

I began to cry because he was slipping away and I didn't want this to happen. I call him and he did not answer. I FaceTime him and he picks up. All I could do was cry. I know he hates when I cry so if it meant anything it will now, he say to me why are you crying baby? And I ask him why he left without telling me? I told you I will be home in 30 minutes. Nicole I love you but you cut me deep and this isn't something I can easily get over. I need my space. Space baby no when you say space things began to happen. Nicole nothing can get any worse than what you did. Stop crying, I told you I'll be home around noon tomorrow. Where are you Kane? In Miami on a business trip. It was last minute and besides I needed to get away because you been at work and not home

with me. Kane (in a crying voice) how am I supposed to know when you won't even look at me. Nicole I'll call you when I get settled in my hotel okay……
Okay baby I love you. Later Nicole. In guess room Kane left his clothes he had on the day before lying on the chair and I grab his shirt and lay across the bed so the smell of his cologne was right there with me. All I could do now was wait for his call because I cannot lose him. I don't know how I was so stupid. AP and I was supposed to hang out the next day but it was no way I was going when Kane was supposed to be back. I waited for his call but he did not call me. I tossed and turned all night so I call Kane he picked up in his voice made me so happy. Kane why didn't you call me? Baby I forgot I started drinking and partying and it slipped my mind. Kane you never forget to call me even when you are drinking and partying. At that

moment I knew things was changing. In the back I can hear the TV so I asked Kane to shut the TV off and he said that's not the TV that's my manager and Justin. I'm all insecure now when Kane never gave me a reason to distrust him. I see we can't talk so I'll see you when you get home. Okay Nicole later. After that call I try and get some sleep so that I am rested for the next day. I called AP to let her know that I won't be in to work tomorrow but if she can still try and find out who told Kane about me cheating and she yells Bitch I already know and she say are you sitting for this and I'm like YES. What you may already can guess and I say who? AP say is Shamar "WHAT" yeah how in the hell he gets around to tell him that. I talked to him last night he comes to my house demanding sex talking about he and you and he aint have no pussy in a month and I asked him and he said the only way I told him if I fucked him. I did it to find out for some answers. Nicole he gave me the whole run down after I fucked him. I hope you are not mad. Naw AP just disappointed. Disappointed at who AP ask, everything. I did a lot of shit for this dude and he want to play me like this. AP you can continue with him if you want maybe that would take his mind off of me. Hell naw Nicole I did that for you. He did say it wasn't over and I tried asking him what that meant but he didn't want to say so be careful because you know how he can get. AP I'm not worried about him because I'm trying to shit right with my man and home and I'll be damned if I let him destroy my relationship. Thanks AP talk to you later okay Hun okay I'll take care of the office. Okay bye. I get my low-key phone and power it on and call Shamar to ask him why he told Kane about me cheating with him and his reply was if I can't have you no one can and I told you that before and I wasn't playing with you. Shamar it was never you and I, we only were Cuddy buddy and you agreed to it. I told you I had a man and now you want to trip me like this. Red you are my bitch so get used to it. No I'm not and stop acting like we are together" it's over and soon I'm turning this phone off for good". I end the call and try to focus on Kane coming home soon. I must get my man back trusting me and now that I know who spilled it so I have to stay away from him.

Chapter 6

Kane called me to let me know he just landed in the Atlanta airport and he should be home within 30 minutes. I was very happy to know he called me to tell me he was on his way. I had already freshen up for him so when he got in it was all about him. When

Tales of a Side Bitch

he walked in the house I kissed him and stick my tongue in his mouth and he pushes me away but I didn't care because he was home and home is where his heart is so I grabbed his jacket and follow him to the guest room and ask him do you want me run some bath water and he said yes. I ran his bath water upstairs because I'm sick of him showering down in the guest room and not to mention sleeping there as well. Baby your water is ready upstairs. He goes upstairs and get into the tub and I wait a half second till I knew he was good. I walk in and start massaging his back and asked him can we talk and he said of course. He is always open to me. I just couldn't believe I went out and cheated on him. That was the stupidest thing I could have done. As we are talking I decided to wash his back and I tell him how sorry I am and that it would never happen again he did not say a word. Kane are you going to say something? You messed up not me so honestly is nothing to say. Will you forgive me? Kane didn't answer so I repeated the question Kane when you forgive me? And he replied and said I'm still here aren't I. That was a big relief. Nicole I don't trust you anymore and you have two gain my trust again. Baby I know and I'm going to do just that. I get in with KANE and sit facing him so that we are eye to eye contact. Kane looks at me like I'm crazy because he didn't want me sexually at that point but I forced him to have sex with me. Is been two weeks too long. I can feel his dick getting hard so I slide it in and ride him real slow Kane leans back and let me take it. I'm making love to him like it was our first time, Kane grabs my lips and slams me on his dick and pushes in real deep. At that point I knew he wanted me as bad as I want to him. The cries I made from the love we made was real and breathtaking. That was special because I love him and I had no doubt that he loves me too. I have stopped taking my birth control because I wanted to have his baby. We had talked about this months ago but it didn't go far because I didn't want any children at that time. Kane was sucking my kitties and telling me you better not give my pussy away again or I'll kill you, I reply Yes Poppie it is yours baby. He whispered give it to me mommy. That was all I needed because I hate when we argue and fight. Later that night Kane rolls over and turn off the clock and turn my phone off. I glance at him and didn't care. I get up the next morning cook breakfast and turn on the TV and the Livingroom and change the channel to the news. There was nothing on the interesting to me. I hear Kane phone ringing and I creep towards the room and all I can make out was Nicole's not coming in today AP so I creep back downstairs and fixed his breakfast and pour him a cup of orange juice. All I wanted to do for the rest of the day was relax and forget about everything because shit was going crazy and none of this would be so if I would have never cheated on Kane or went to that damn meeting. He is a good man and I messed up.

Baby I have been doing a lot of thinking and I want to know how you feel about me selling my business? I want you to really feel like that is what you want to do and not for me or anyone else. Kane it is for me and I thought about it long and hard. I'm thinking next year and focus on other things. Nicole if this is what you really want, but I think you should keep it and let AP run it full time by herself. Let it work for you instead of you going in each day. Just let AP run or be the co-owner you let AP be the owner. I wouldn't just let it go. Maybe I'll think about it. I really don't want to stress about it anymore. It is making great money right now and that is a good thing

Now that Kane and I on the role to getting things back to where they were. I still have Lexi on my mind and if the police has connected any of our phones timeline or anything that could have them wanted to question me or AP

It was Wednesday 545 in the evening and I was still at the office finishing up some paperwork. Everyone was gone and all the calls was forwarded to the company's voicemail. Suddenly all the lights gold out I get up to check the other office to see if the power was out and it was. I am walking through the hall

hallway and all of a sudden I hear a big boom and

smoke. My heart dropped and I began to panic. It was

the FBI raiding my shit. I was thrown to the floor and

handcuffed. The police asked who was there with me

and I replied no one he rolls me over so that I can sit

up and it was a voice that I had heard before but

wasn't sure because his face was covered. I could not

say a word because I was lost about why was it my

place of business being rated. The officer continued

to question me but for some reason no words will

come out. I soon realized who was behind the mask it

was Amar. All I could do was ask myself why?

Because it did not make any sense to me. The

detective took six big bags out of my business and

four of my computers. I wasn't worried because they

had nothing on it and the throwaway phone was off

and locked up in my basement at my house, but I was worried that they was going to hit my house or did they already. Kane is going to flip when he finds out about this shit. I wanted to kill Shamar at this point because he was using me all along and now it all makes sense why he wasn't worried about Lexi.

The next day my bond was set at $55,000. Kane bailed me out and all I could do was cry when I saw him. Nicole they got. AP to and Trenton. Nicole you need to talk to me and tell me everything because they shit is real. They have you down as racketeering really Nicole Kane reply. I can't believe you. All this going on and you for looking out like this you know I don't like the police and here you are bringing it to our home. Kane is yelling and all I could do was sit there because I fucked up bad and all the secrets are coming back to haunt me. My bank account is frozen so bonding AP out was out of the question. I look at Kane asking what about AP Kane yells what about her Nicole? I already knew what was next so I couldn't do anything but put my head down. Kane yells she got a man don't she........ I didn't say anything so Kane repeat itself don't she Nicole I reply in a baby voice no baby she doesn't. We pull up in the driveway Kane gets out without even thinking twice of me and heads into the house. AP was on my mind because she is my best friend and I couldn't just let her sit there. I called out to the jail and the woman on the other in end said bail was posted on her and all I could do was ask myself who???? I heard you hang up the phone and go upstairs and Kane has moved all of his stuff out of the room to the guest room downstairs. All I could do was cry because it was hard on him when he found out I was cheating. Life is full of lessons and this is one that I sure have learned a lesson from. When AP got out she did not call me to pick her up. I was very worried because she does not have a man. The only person that crossed my mind that could have picked her up was Shamar. At that point a million things crossed my mind because he is the police and I pray that she is not working for him now to set me up. She is my best friend and I would never turn on her but I knew she is thinking that I didn't want to bond her out or coming to get her. I must talk to her so that I can explain it all to her. I tried phoning her but she kept sending me to voicemail. I grabbed my keys and went over to her joint to see her. She was not there. At this point I'm very wary because this is not like her at all. I want to go by Shamars but I do not want to see the answer to that if she is there. I head over to Shamar and her car is parked in the driveway so I let myself in the gate and ring the doorbell and no answer so I bang on the door still no answer. My phone is going off because Kane is calling me but right now I can't talk to him because I have to find AP. I'm riding every spot that I can think of where AP could be but she is not in neither places. It is now 8 PM and still no word from AP. Kane is very upset with me and my best friend is nowhere to be found. Everything is falling apart. I'm cooking dinner and Kane's in the guest room with the door shut and this is not him closing doors. I did not know if I should knock or go in. I turned the knob and the doors locked. I knocked softly he yells in a loud voice "What Cole" are you eating dinner? No. Please baby I responded no Cole go ahead and eat dinner I'll eat later. I walk away a fix my dinner. I wrapped his plate and places in the microwave. AP calls and I tell her to come over to the house and she explained she can't. I asked why she just hangs up the phone. I hang up and turn off my phone and finish up my dinner and take a shower. The next morning I'm getting ready to go to the office and Kane's already gone. Kane knew what was going on but didn't say anything to me because he wanted me to come to him to talk about it. AP never showed up to the office and I cannot understand any of the madness that was going on because I was always there for AP and now I'm losing the man of that I love and my best friend.

What happens when Kane finds out that his woman Nicole is cheating with Atlanta Biggest drug ring

Tales of a Side Bitch

leader at least she thought he was until her million-
dollar business is raided by the FBI and she later
learns that Shamar was the police all along. AP her
best friend are sleeping with the same guy and later
learns that Shamar is AP baby daddy

Cover design Casey Diggs